Dinosaur Family Trip

By May Nakamura
Based on the television series created by Craig Bartlett

Ready-to-Read

SIMON SPOTLIGHT
New York London Toronto Sydney New Delhi

Here is a list of all the words you will find in this book. Sound them out before you begin reading the story.

Names:

Buddy

Dad

Shiny

SIMON SPOTLIGHT

An imprint of Simon & Schuster Children's Publishing Division · 1230 Avenue of the Americas, New York, New York 10020 · This Simon Spotlight edition September 2019
© 2019 The Jim Henson Company. JIM HENSON'S mark & logo, DINOSAUR TRAIN mark & logo, characters and elements are trademarks of The Jim Henson Company. All Rights Reserved.
All rights reserved, including the right of reproduction in whole or in part in any form.
SIMON SPOTLIGHT, READY-TO-READ, and colophon are registered trademarks of Simon & Schuster, Inc.
For information about special discounts for bulk purchases, please contact Simon & Schuster Special Sales at 1-866-506-1949 or business@simonandschuster.com. · Manufactured in the United States of America 0719 LAK
2 4 6 8 10 9 7 5 3 1 · ISBN 978-1-5344-3984-9 (hc) · ISBN 978-1-5344-3983-2 (pbk) · ISBN 978-1-5344-3985-6 (eBook)

Word families:

"-ay"	→	day	play
"-es"	→	best	rest
"-oat"	→	boat	float

Sight words:

a	all	and	big
can	fly	go	his
is	on	read	ride
see	some	that	the
they	this	too	water
will	with		

Bonus words:

animals	dinosaurs	family	great
sky	swim	trip	

Ready to go? Happy reading!

Don't miss the questions about the story
on the last page of this book.

This is Buddy.

This is Buddy and his family.

They will go on a trip.

They ride on a boat.

The boat can float.

Some dinosaurs rest.

Some dinosaurs play.

Dad will fly
with Buddy.
Shiny will fly too.

They see the sky.

They see animals that fly.

They see the water.

They see animals
that swim.

The family trip is great.

GROWN-UPS, READ THESE PAGES WITH YOUR CHILD IF THEY'D LIKE TO LEARN MORE ABOUT BOATS.

Bonus information about paddle wheels and rivers!

The dinosaur boat has a paddle wheel that goes around and around, just like the wheels on a train. The paddle wheel pushes the water and moves the boat forward.

Every river has a current, which is the way that the water flows. The direction of the current is called "downstream." The opposite direction of the current is called "upstream." Without a paddle wheel, the dinosaur boat would not be able to travel upstream!

DOWNSTREAM

UPSTREAM

Now that you have read the story, can you answer these questions?

1. What do Buddy and his family ride on?

2. Who flies with Buddy and Dad?

3. In this story, you read the words "boat" and "float." These words rhyme. Can you think of other words that rhyme with "boat" and "float"?

Great job!
You are a reading star!